DrRoach

First published in Great Britain in 2012 by Boxer Books Limited.

www.boxerbooks.com

Based on an original idea by Sam Williams.

Monstrous Stories™ concept, names, stories, designs and logos
© Boxer Books Limited

Written by Paul Harrison
Paul Harrison asserts his moral right to be identified
as the author of this work.
Text copyright © 2012 Boxer Books Limited

Illustrated by Tom Knight
Tom Knight asserts his moral right to be identified
as the illustrator of this work.
Illustrations copyright © 2012 Tom Knight

The illustrations were prepared using brush, ink and digital.
The text is set in Blackmoor Plain and Adobe Caslon.

ISBN 978-1-907967-35-1
1 3 5 7 9 10 8 6 4 2

Printed and bound by CPI Group (UK) Ltd, Croydon, CR0 4YY

All of our papers are sourced from managed forests and renewable resources.

Dr Roach's
Monstrous
STORIES

Dr Roach presents

FROGOSAURUS vs. THE BOG MONSTER

a Boxer Books production

Contents

5

Dr Roach welcomes YOU!

Do you have a favourite place? Sammy and Tammy do. They love the quiet boggy marshes full of insects and strange plants.

Meet Maximus Sneer. An evil man with lots of money and a secret plan. He is going to drain the boggy marshes dry. Then build houses and shops and car parks.

But instead of creating homes he creates two giant monsters–without even knowing it.

How, you ask? Come closer, my friend, and I'll tell you all about it.

Welcome to Dr Roach's Monstrous Stories. Enjoy!

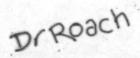

Chapter 1
Stinky Bog

Sammy Linnet stretched out his fishing net over the stinky, brown waters of the boggy marshes.

"Give me your hand," said Sammy to his twin sister Tammy, "and then I can reach that deep pool."

"Careful," said Tammy, grabbing him as he leaned out.

"Nearly there," said
Sammy. "Just a little bit
further …"
"HEY YOU!"
The man's voice
was a shock. Tammy
screamed and let go of her
brother's hand. Sammy hovered

in mid-air, waving his arms like
windmills as he tried to stay balanced
– then toppled face first into the bog
with a gloopy SPLURCH!

"Euurrggghhh," said Tammy,
as Sammy struggled to get up, all
covered in mud and slime. "You look
like a bog monster!"

"Oh, very funny. Now help me out," Sammy replied.

"Not a chance—that mud stinks!" said Tammy, taking a step backwards.

"Hey, you two!"

An angry man was standing behind them. He was the size and shape of a dresser, but in this case the dresser was wearing a bright yellow parka with SECURITY written on the back.

"What are you two doing?" he asked.

"We're collecting samples for our school science project," said Tammy. "There are lots of really rare animals and plants living here and ..."

"Yeah? Well, not for much longer. This is private property now," said the man.

"Private property?" spluttered Sammy. "Since when?"

"Since Maximus Sneer bought it. Now clear off!"

Tammy and Sammy walked and squelched their way home, past men building a high fence around the boggy marshes.

"What does Maximus Sneer want with the boggy marshes?" said Tammy.

"I don't know, but they've always been open to the public. He can't just fence them off!" said Sammy.

"You're right," Tammy agreed. "We should organise a protest or something."

"Great idea! Let's do it now," Sammy suggested.

"No," Tammy replied, holding her nose, "let's do it after you've had a bath."

Chapter 2
Maximus Sneer

Maximus Sneer sat behind a large
desk in his headquarters. In front of
him, a large screen on the wall was
showing plans for new buildings on
the boggy marshes. A knock at the
door disturbed Sneer's thoughts.

"Come in!" barked Sneer. "Ah,
Perkins, what news?"

"The draining work has started, Mr
Sneer," Perkins replied.

"And the water is being pumped into the old quarry?" Sneer asked.

"Yes, sir – just as you ordered," replied the man.

"Excellent, Perkins, excellent!"

"If I may be so bold, sir, don't we need permission to drain the marshes?" Perkins asked.

"Maximus Sneer does not ask permission for anything!" snapped Sneer.

He slammed his fist on a large button and a huge screen rose, revealing a large window that flooded the room with daylight. The window offered a view of the boggy marshes.

"Look at that, Perkins. Those marshes are nothing but mud and water! But soon they will be houses, shops, cinemas and car parks. And they will all be mine!

And when people live there … they'll
be mine. And then I shall take over
the world!"

"The world, sir?" asked Perkins.

"Did I say world?" Sneer replied.

"Yes, sir, you did."

Across town, Sammy and Tammy were putting the finishing touches to their protest plans.

"So what do you think?" asked Tammy, holding up signs with the words Save Our Bog painted on.

"Great!" replied Sammy. "And I've put up posters telling people what's going on. There should be a good crowd for tomorrow's protest!"

"Yeah, let's hope so – we need something big to get Sneer's attention," said Tammy.

They were certainly going to get that.

Chapter 3
It's ALIVE!

The water from Sneer's pumps gushed into the old quarry and trickled down through the rocks. Then drip, drip, drip it went, into an underground cave and onto a large dried-up lump in the middle. The lump soaked up the water like a sponge, until something remarkable happened. It opened its eyes.

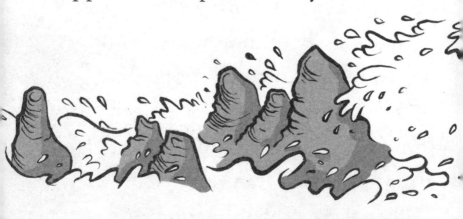

Frogosaurus was ALIVE!

Who knows how long Frogosaurus had been trapped in the cave – a long time, that's for sure. It blinked its big bulgy eyes and looked around. With a dry cracking sound, it opened its mouth and a long dry tongue stretched out to catch the drips of water. Slowly it stretched its froggy back legs and flexed its arm-like front legs and gave itself a shake. Then Frogosaurus took a deep breath and for the first time in thousands of years gave its fearsome roar once again:

"Ribbit."

Frogosaurus gave a cough and tried once more. And this time it was thunderous: "RRRRIIIIIIIB BBBBBBBBBIIIIIIIIIIT TTTTTTTT!"

Meanwhile, back in Sneer's headquarters, Maximus Sneer looked up from his smartphone.

"Perkins, did you hear something just then?" he asked.

"No, sir," Perkins replied.

"Hmm, strange," said Sneer, returning to his master plan, "very strange."

In the boggy marshes, the
disappearing water was leaving
thick, gloopy mud. The mud
squished together and made lumps
and bumps. The lumps and bumps
became clumps, and then heaps and
mounds, and slowly squidged itself

together to form
a big slimy mass.
For the second
time that day,
something
remarkable happened – the mound
of mud opened its eyes.

The mound began to move and a
wibbly tower of mud rose into the
air, slime slipping from the surface
as it swayed from side to side. Two
great muddy limbs
appeared, followed
by two great legs.

It saw the water
draining away.

The Bog
Monster thought
of revenge!

Chapter 4
The Bog Monster Cometh!

Maximus Sneer sat scowling in the back seat of his luxury car.

"What on earth is taking so long, Perkins?" he barked at the driver.

"I'm sorry, Mr Sneer, sir, but there seems to be some kind of demonstration up ahead," Perkins replied. "They're blocking the way into the marshes."

Sneer peered through the window. He could see a group of people waving signs and chanting.

"Pull over, Perkins! I'll deal with this!" shouted Sneer.

"Now, what is the meaning of this?" he barked as he flung open the door. "Who is in charge here?"

"We are," said Tammy and Sammy.

"Very amusing, now who's really in

28

charge?" said Sneer.

"We are," said the twins again. "And we want you to leave the boggy marshes alone."

"Oh, this is priceless!" said Sneer, a thin smile splitting his wicked face. "Two junior mud huggers. Well, let me tell you, Tweedle Dee and Tweedle Dum, or whatever your names are, you can't stop me because I represent business and you are children."

He spat out the last word like it tasted of something horrible.

"But we're not moving!" cried Tammy. "These marshes are special—they are home to loads of different plants and animals."

"Mr Sneer, sir," said Perkins.

"Oh, please," said Sneer. "It's full of mud, slugs and weeds. Name just one amazing thing that comes from that bog."

"Mr Sneer, sir," repeated Perkins anxiously. "Look!"

In the distance was a great
swaying tower of mud,
twenty storeys high,
slowly slurping
across the
ground.

For a couple of seconds the crowd watched amazed as Bog Monster squelched towards them.

"It's going to get us!" someone shouted. Screaming, the crowd ran off in panic – even the police officers.

"Perkins!" Sneer cried. "Get me out of here! *Now!*"

RIALTO

NIGHT OF THE ZOMBIE GOLDFISH

Chapter 5
Frogosaurus Arrives

Maximus Sneer dived into his car and with a squeal of tyres was gone. Only Tammy and Sammy were left.

"What's that?" exclaimed Sammy.

"I don't know – it looks like the bog has got up and moved," replied Tammy.

"Yeah – and we'd better do the same," said Sammy.

"Hold on a minute – what's that sound?" said Tammy, grabbing her brother's arm. There was a noise like someone speaking, but from a long way away.

"It's the police radio," said Sammy, pointing at the squad car that had been left when the police had run off. The radio was repeating a message.

"Attention all units! Back-up required immediately! Old quarry area a ... a ... monster has appeared. This is not a joke. I repeat, this is not a joke! We have mass panic on our hands here. We need help – urgently!"

"The old quarry? That's miles away!" said Tammy.

"So there are two monsters now?" said Sammy. "This I've got to see – let's go!"

In between the boggy marshes and the old quarry were Maximus Sneer's headquarters. Sneer's car squealed to a halt outside.

"Quick, Perkins," said Sneer as he got out of the car. "I want you to get

the police on the phone–no, the army–and make sure that monster is dealt with. It's going to ruin my plans!"

"And what would you like me to do about THAT?" asked Perkins, pointing behind Sneer, his face white with fear.

"What are you blathering about?" snapped Sneer.

Then he saw what Perkins could see –

Frogosaurus!

An enormous half frog, half human thing with giant bug eyes and a flicking tongue was leaping across the ground in gigantic bounds, straight towards them.

"Perkins!" cried Sneer. "Get me my mummy!"

Chapter 6
Mud Fight

Thirty seconds later, Bog Monster arrived. And he spotted Frogosaurus. It was hate at first sight – there was room for only one monster here, and neither was going to back down.

Frogosaurus leapt at Bog Monster in one massive bound and slammed into it with a huge SQUELCH!

Bog Monster instantly changed
shape and became a giant hand that
swatted Frogosaurus aside with a
soggy slap. The giant frog beast was
sent tumbling backwards – right into
Maximus Sneer's headquarters. Bog
Monster built itself into a huge wave
of mud and crashed into the building
after Frogosaurus.

The next moment, Frogosaurus had leapt through the roof in an explosion of bricks, chairs, tables and pot plants. It twisted in mid-air and landed back on top of Bog Monster in another wild attack, mud flying everywhere. Frogosaurus

bounded from side to side, grabbing with its wiry arms and stabbing with its flicking tongue. Bog Monster constantly changed shape trying to catch it.

A line of police officers outside the building kept the crowd of onlookers – including Tammy and Sammy – at a safe distance.

"Perkins, I demand that you do something!" shouted Sneer hysterically. He and Perkins were

 now so
completely
covered in
dirt that they
looked like
snowmen made of mud.

"I will do something," Perkins
replied. "I'm going to quit!"

And with that he stalked off. Sneer
turned to the police officers.

"Stop them! They're destroying my
lovely building," Sneer whined.

"I'm afraid there's
not much we can
do," a police
sergeant
explained.
"Typical!
If you want

something done, you've got to do it yourself!" snapped Sneer. He grabbed a loud hailer from one of the officers.

"You two!" Sneer shouted at the monsters. "You are trespassing on my property! Leave now!"

The monsters stopped mid-fight and slowly turned to look at Sneer. Evil grins split their faces and they started to move towards him.

"Oh dear ..." whispered Sneer. "Mummy ..."

Chapter 7
Brainwave

As soon as the monsters changed direction the crowd scattered. In one giant bound, Frogosaurus was among them, with Bog Monster sloshing up behind. People were screaming and panicking, dashing this way and that. Fortunately, the two monsters had difficulty choosing who to chase, and the people were too small to grab easily. Cars got squashed and buildings got smashed as Frogosaurus and Bog Monster went on the rampage.

"We've got to do something," shouted Tammy.

"But what?" said Sammy.

"I've got an idea," Tammy replied. "They're from the marshes, right? Think about our science project – what's bad for the marshes?"

"Erm, too much heat or water can kill off a lot of the life that's there," said Sammy.

"And that's exactly what we've got to give the monsters," said Tammy. "We give the gloopy one so much water that it makes it too weak to pull itself together. The other one looks drier, so we should try to dry it out completely."

"You're a genius!" said Sammy.

"I know," Tammy replied. "Now, let's get started."

The twins quickly explained their idea to the police sergeant, and the plan swung into action.

Frogosaurus bounded into the town square. There were people all around the edges and, oddly, they all had barbecues. Frogosaurus didn't care.

It licked its lips and decided who to snatch first. It was beginning to feel uncomfortably warm, but there were so many people to chase that Frogosaurus ignored the heat.

It stretched out an arm and there was a terrible CRACK! Frogosaurus

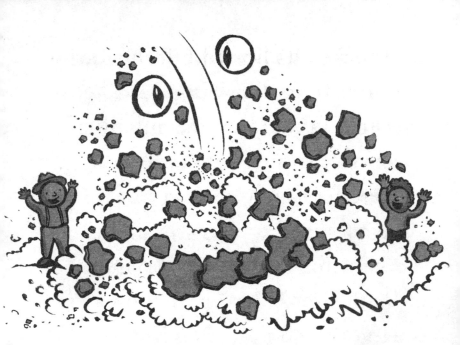

was drying out – it needed water and fast. It stumbled around the square looking for an escape route.

There was none. It was barbecues all round. Finally, Frogosaurus tried to leap the ring of fire, but its legs had dried out and completely lost their spring. Instead it crashed to the ground – shattering into thousands of dry, crusty pieces.

The crowd cheered but the job was only half done. Bog Monster hovered in the distance, lurching from side to side in the ruins of Sneer's headquarters in a threatening manner.

"Now for Stage 2!" said Sammy.

With sirens blaring, the town's fire engines raced past. Bog Monster

looked confused and
distracted by the noise
and lights. It did the only thing it
could think of—attack! It rose high
like a giant wave of mud ready to
crash down on the fire engines below.
But the water from the hoses hit Bog
Monster first, sending it wheeling
backwards. It tried swatting the

water away but with no luck.

A huge pool of dirt began to form around the bottom of Bog Monster, who swayed this way and that trying to avoid the high-powered jets.

Slowly, the flailing monster got smaller and the puddle got bigger, seeping and spreading across the ground, flooding the ruined building. With one last, desperate attack, Bog Monster hurled itself at the fire engines, but splattered on

the ground in a shower of mud a
good way short of its target.

The monsters were no more.
Tammy and Sammy reached the
ruined headquarters just as
Bog Monster came to his
gloopy end.
"So that's that," said
Tammy.

Suddenly, a small mound of mud rose from the ground. A quick blast from a hose sent it flying backwards.

"Stop! Stop!" spluttered Maximus

Sneer. "It's me!"

He stood sad and soggy among the boggy wasteland that had been his headquarters.

"You've learned a valuable lesson today, Mr Sneer," said Sammy.

"What's that? Don't mess with

nature?" Sneer replied.

"No," said Sammy. "If you're going
to have a barbecue, always have some
water close at hand, just in case."

The only person who didn't laugh
was Maximus Sneer.

What can make all the mice in a small town suddenly stand still?

A giant cheese? A huge mousetrap? No - a flying saucer from outer space!

Alien cats have come to Earth in search of an endless supply of fresh milk. They are shrinking all the cows and are ready to fly off with them.

Will the alien cats pull off their purr-fect plan? Will the cows be making mini-moos? Will someone stop them? Jilly McCafferty will- because she also has a plan.

Get a copy today and I'll tell you everything!

Catch you later!

Dr Roach